My
Great-grandmother's
Gourd

My Great-Grandmother's Gourd

by CRISTINA KESSLER

illustrated by WALTER LYON KRUDOP

Orchard Books   New York

To all my Sudanese friends who helped me, especially Jerimico,
Daw, and Ahmed, as well as to my best friend and husband, Joe.
And to all the great baobab trees that give shade in the day,
shelter in the rain, and water in the dry season.—C.K.

To Benjamin—W.L.K.

Text copyright © 2000 by Cristina Kessler
Illustrations copyright © 2000 by Walter Lyon Krudop

Orchard Books, A Grolier Company
95 Madison Avenue, New York, NY 10016

Manufactured in the United States of America
Printed and bound by Phoenix Color Corp. Book design by Barbara Powderly
The text of this book is set in 14 point Berkeley Bold. The illustrations are oil paint.

10 9 8 7 6 5 4 3 2 1

Library of Congress Cataloging-in-Publication Data
Kessler, Cristina.
My great-grandmother's gourd / by Cristina Kessler ;
illustrated by Walter Lyon Krudop.
p.   cm.
Summary: Residents of a Sudanese village rejoice when a traditional
water storage method is replaced by modern technology, but Fatima's grandmother
knows there is no substitute for the reliability of the baobab tree.
ISBN 0-531-30284-9 (tr. : alk. paper)
ISBN 0-531-33284-5 (lib. bdg. : alk. paper)
[1. Grandmothers—Fiction. 2. Water—Fiction. 3. Sudan—Fiction.]
I. Krudop, Walter, date, ill. II. Title.
PZ7.K4824 My 2000 [E]—dc21 99-56553

Arabic Words

Haboob (ha-BOOB)—The strong winds that blow down off the
    Sahara every May and June, just before the rainy season.

Inshallah (in-SHA-allah)—God or Allah willing. Used constantly.

Khalas (kha-LAS)—Finished. Said like "the end."

Malesh (ma-LESH)—Sorry. Used all the time.

Shukran (SHOOK-ran)—Thank you.

Tabaldi (ta-BELL-di)—Local name for baobab tree.

Towb (tope)—Long, colorful cloth that women wrap around
    their heads and bodies.

I'll always remember the first day the blue pump worked. The men in their turbans and the women in their *towbs* laughed and chattered as the bright, shining pump was fixed on top of the old well.

"Imagine," said Ibrahim, the village chief, "no more camels pulling water for drinking and washing and cooking. No more filling of the old trees to get us through the dry season. Progress has come to our village."

Ahmed, the barber, called out, "Who shall take the first pump of this fancy new machine?"

Silence filled the air until Hanan, the neighbor, said, "Let it be a child, to show just how easy it will be. Fatima, you pump and we will watch the water flow. *Inshallah.*"

I stepped to the long handle, so hard and smooth in my hand, and pulled down. A soft creaking noise filled the silence. Everyone watched without speaking a word. But not a drop fell.

I pulled again, and a second soft *creeeeak* was surrounded by stillness—something rare in our village. Out gushed a stream of clear water. As if a spell had been broken, a sudden cheer filled the air and drums began beating.

Was it for me or the water? I wondered. I looked for my grandmother, who always says she is so proud of me, but I didn't see her face in the excited crowd. As people pushed forward to try the pump, I pushed outward to find my grandmother.

There she stood all alone beneath her best friend, an old baobab tree. I rushed to her, caught up in the drumbeats welcoming the pump.

"Grandmother, come see the new pump. The water is so easy to get now, our work will be less. Come dance."

I could see my friends and cousins dancing with arms flung wide. Turning circles, they kicked up small dust devils around their feet. I wanted to dance, too, for the drumbeat was powerful and the excitement was calling me.

Grandmother looked at me, then patted the gnarled trunk of the giant baobab tree with her work-worn hand and said, "Go dance, child. Drink the fresh, cold water. And soon I'll be there too."

I ran back and danced with my friends, celebrating the new pump. But my grandmother did not come.

Every morning I raced the girls of the village to the pump. The first one there got to pull down the long, shimmering handle for as long as she wanted, filling buckets and tins, head pans and gourds. I raced to the well each day, hoping to be the first.

My grandmother spent more and more time with her friend the baobab. Leaning against its great trunk. Resting beneath its wide-reaching shadow. Watching the girls and women walk to and from the well. Watching and waiting for what, I didn't know.

Early one evening, after the food had been eaten and the sun's heat was only a whisper on my skin, I joined my grandmother beneath the tree.

Grandmother took my hand and placed it on the ancient bark of the giant trunk. She didn't say a word, but her sadness was loud.

"Tell me, Grandmother, what makes you so sad?" I asked as I looked deep into her eyes. "Is it the pump? Don't you like it?"

With tired eyes she looked at me and said, "The rains are nearly here, and still no one works to prepare the trees. All the years of my life, drumbeats would fill the village, and voices would sing and chant as we all worked together. But now there's only the *creeak, creeak* of metal. And no one works together, or works at all, to prepare the trees."

Gently patting the trunk, she said, "I always called this my great-grandmother's gourd. The name my grandmother called it. And her grandmother before her."

I smoothed the *towb* around her wrinkled face and said, "But, Grandmother, with the pump we don't need the trees. The days of storing water in trees are past."

She let go of my hand.

"Grandmother," I said, "that was then and this is now."

I couldn't sleep that night, for the air seemed heavy, so I sat outside. The moon cast great pools of darkness across the flat landscape. I was thinking about my stubborn grandmother, when, silent as a shadow, she sat down beside me.

I gazed upon our family's only baobab and let my eyes wander up the tree to the scrawny branches. Each branch looked small and separate in the light of the moon.

As if she read my mind, Grandmother said softly, "She gives us shade in the day. Shelter in the rain. And water in the dry season. She is the tree of life."

"No, Grandmother, the baobab will give us shade in the day and shelter in the rain. *Khalas*. And the pump will give us water in the dry season."

Shaking her head, she said, "Good-night, Granddaughter," and walked back to our hut.

I rose that next day with the first rays of the sun, when the air was still cool. Dressing quickly, I rushed to the well to pump away all the questions that my old-fashioned grandmother stirred in me.

I was first and I pumped till my shoulders ached. *Creeak, creeak* sang the pump. Nagla, the neighbor who always had something to say, called out, "Fatima is pumping like a woodpecker hammering a tree, and she fills your bucket before it is settled on the ground."

A long line of girls, with brimming buckets and tins, head pans and gourds balanced on their heads, streamed back and forth between the huts and the pump.

The hut was empty when I returned. I looked toward our field to find Grandmother. Instead, I saw her bent over her hoe at the base of her baobab tree.

I ran to her and shouted, "Grandmother, people will laugh at you, preparing your tree." I wanted to take the hoe from her hands, but she stood straight and said to me in a voice as hard as the dry earth, "Some may laugh. What do I care? I have work to do."

She worked in silence, for as the sun rose the heat was great. *Creak, creak* sang the pump. *Hack, hack* went my grandmother's hoe. Working alone, she looked as thin as one of the tree's skinny branches.

"Can I help?" I asked.

"No," she said. She wiped the sweat dripping from her brow with the end of her *towb* and bent back to her work.

One day Ahmed, the barber, passed our tree and shouted with a laugh, "For some people new ideas are like puddles on the clay: they never sink in."

Balgeese, the midwife, called out, "To fight progress is to fight the wind, old woman. Come, let's go to the pump."

But Grandmother kept right on working. Her back bent over her hoe, she was slowly digging out what looked like a large necklace around the base of the baobab's trunk.

Another day Nagla, the neighbor who never stops talking, passed. With

a voice louder than the call to prayer, she said, "Who but a fool makes extra work? Myself, I use the well." Then she laughed. And I realized she was laughing at my grandmother. Old-fashioned or not, *my* grandmother.

I nearly knocked Nagla down as I grabbed my hoe and ran to the tree. Without a word, I started digging beside my grandmother. We worked side by side.

For days we dug, deepening the circle around the trunk. We didn't talk. In peaceful silence, we shared the work of my grandmother's great-grandmother.

People passed us, but now no one said a word. They still looked at us from the sides of their faces, balancing buckets and head pans, pots and gourds full of water on their heads. We worked on.

Creak, creak went the blue pump.

One day as the sun dipped below the earth's edge, Grandmother put away her hoe. "Now," she said, "we must wait for the rains."

The first rain comes as fiercely as the first winds of the *haboob.* Grandmother and I stood in it, feeling the water dripping down our faces. We watched our necklace around the giant old tree's trunk slowly fill with water. The parched earth turned a shiny red as the giant raindrops plopped upon it.

When the rain stopped, I climbed the tree and sat by a small hole at the top of the trunk. The hole that had been made by my grandmother's great-grandmother's great-grandmother.

I dropped the bucket tied to my waist down to Grandmother, who filled it to its brim from the baobab's necklace. Slowly I pulled the bucket up, then poured its contents into the tree. It took two breaths before we heard the splash of water hitting bottom, deep inside the tree. Grandmother's eyes sparkled at the old, familiar sound.

Ahmed, the barber, passed by, and, shaking his head in wonder, said, "I guess some people like extra work." But we took no notice of him as the sweet splash of water rose higher and higher inside the old tree.

Day after day now, I climbed the tree, and Grandmother filled the bucket. We worked together, filling our tree. Finally, when the rains ended, the tree was full.

The scorching dry season came early. Each day the horizon danced where the shimmering blue sky met the earth's baking red clay. Lines formed at the well, and the girls in their colorful *towbs* looked like a python stretched across the desert floor sunning itself. As the temperatures rose, people made many more trips to the well.

From the first rays of light till the sky glowed hot, red, and dusty as the sun slipped away, people pumped. The steady *creeak, creeak* turned to *screech! screech!* as people pumped water from sunup to sunset.

And then one day the pump stopped.

"We will fix it," said the chief, Ibrahim. Omar, the baker, and Musa, the butcher, brought out all the tools needed to take the pump off the well. People stood about in silence, waiting for the news.

Musa pulled a large metal piece, sharp along one edge, from the pump's neck. "It has broken clean, from too much use. *Malesh,*" he said to the quiet crowd. "I don't know what we shall do, for I have no spare part like this."

The men passed the broken metal rod from hand to hand in silence, each examining its sharp edge. "I will make another piece," said Boubacar, the cart builder. "But it will take some days."

"How can we wait days?" cried Nagla. "What shall we do without water?"

"We go back to the old ways," said Ahmed. "We shall use the camels to pull the water out of the well, just like in days past." Then he looked straight at my grandmother and told Nagla, "And two smart villagers can use their tree."

"This year we will share our tree," said Grandmother. "Maybe it's wise to mix old with new. We shall see."

Ahmed looked at her a moment, then nodded his head yes. He turned to the two men and said, "Get the camels and ropes."

His son, Abu Bakar, called to his friends Ali, Salah, and Osman, "Get the buckets. We'll go to the tree."

With great pride I said, "Yes! To my great-grandmother's gourd."

And before the next rainy season came, the village throbbed with the beating of drums and the chants of singing voices. The people worked together, preparing the trees for the rains, just in case the pump broke again.

I looked at Grandmother, whose smile shone brighter than the African sun, and said, "Remember last year? The silence and laughter as we worked alone?"

"Yes," she said. "But that was then and this is now."

And each day I pat the old baobab's trunk and say, "*Shukran*, my friend, for you give us shade in the day, shelter in the rain, and water in the dry season."

"One day you will be my great-granddaughter's gourd."

Author's Note

In the North Kordafan area of Sudan, in East Africa, there is a place called "The Thirst Triangle." It's called that because the ground there is a very hard red clay. When the rains fall each year, very little water seeps into the ground because of this hard red clay. This means it's very difficult to have water year round. Fortunately, there are giant trees called baobabs, or *tabaldi* in Arabic.

For centuries, people have been using these great old trees as giant water gourds. This is a story about how a traditional water storage method is being replaced by modern technology. In an effort to help, several different foreign organizations have come into the area and dug wells that are very, very deep.

The story is based on a true event. As people became more dependent on the wells, they became less inclined to fill their trees. One season of poor rains, a faulty well, and a great thirst changed that. As Fatima's grandmother says, "Maybe it's wise to mix old with new."

By combining the two, life is better for all.